GOD'S WONDERFUL COLORING BOOK

DEEP SEA CREATURES

MW01047987

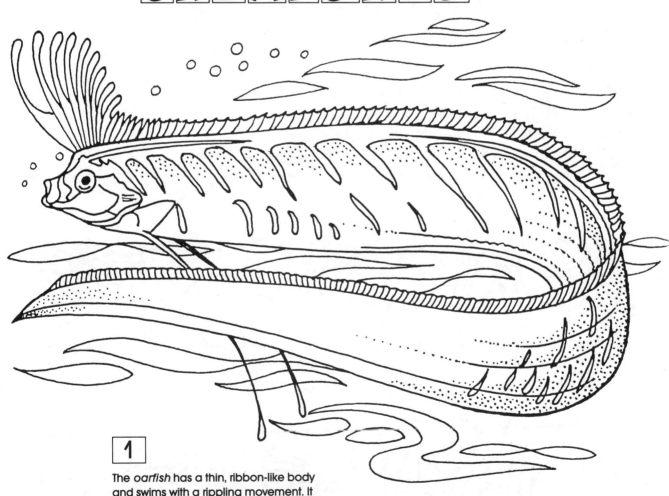

1

The *oarfish* has a thin, ribbon-like body and swims with a rippling movement. It can grow up to 7m (23ft) long! There are no teeth in the oarfish's small mouth and it feeds on tiny creatures like shrimps.

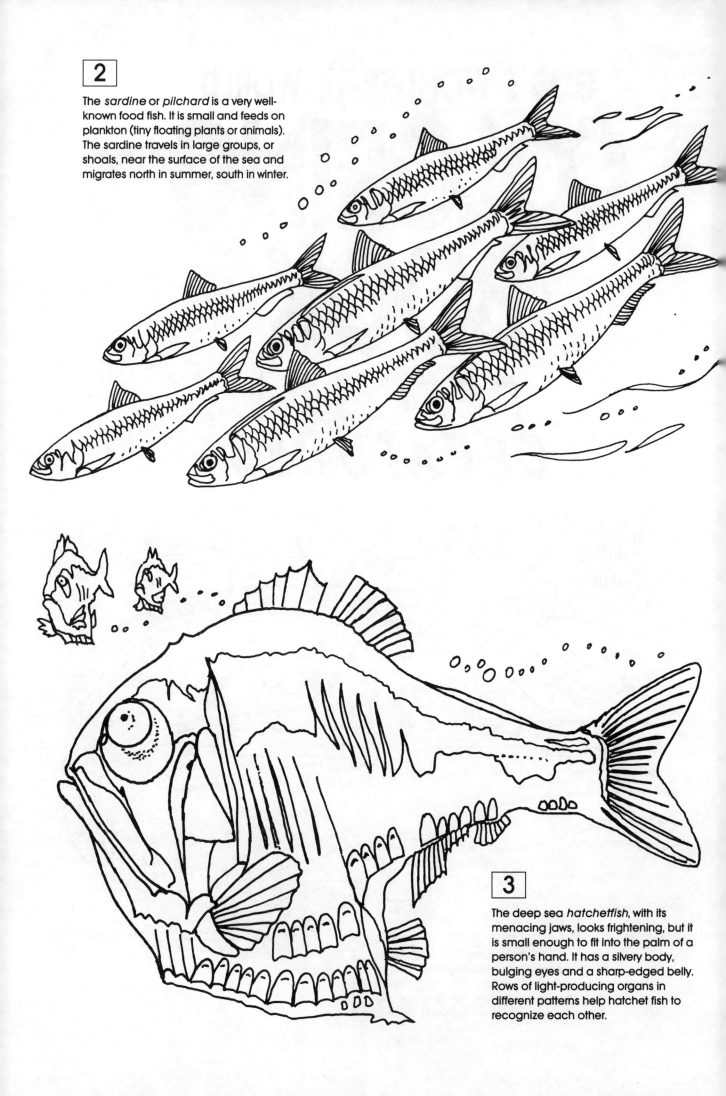

2

The *sardine* or *pilchard* is a very well-known food fish. It is small and feeds on plankton (tiny floating plants or animals). The sardine travels in large groups, or shoals, near the surface of the sea and migrates north in summer, south in winter.

3

The deep sea *hatchetfish*, with its menacing jaws, looks frightening, but it is small enough to fit into the palm of a person's hand. It has a silvery body, bulging eyes and a sharp-edged belly. Rows of light-producing organs in different patterns help hatchet fish to recognize each other.

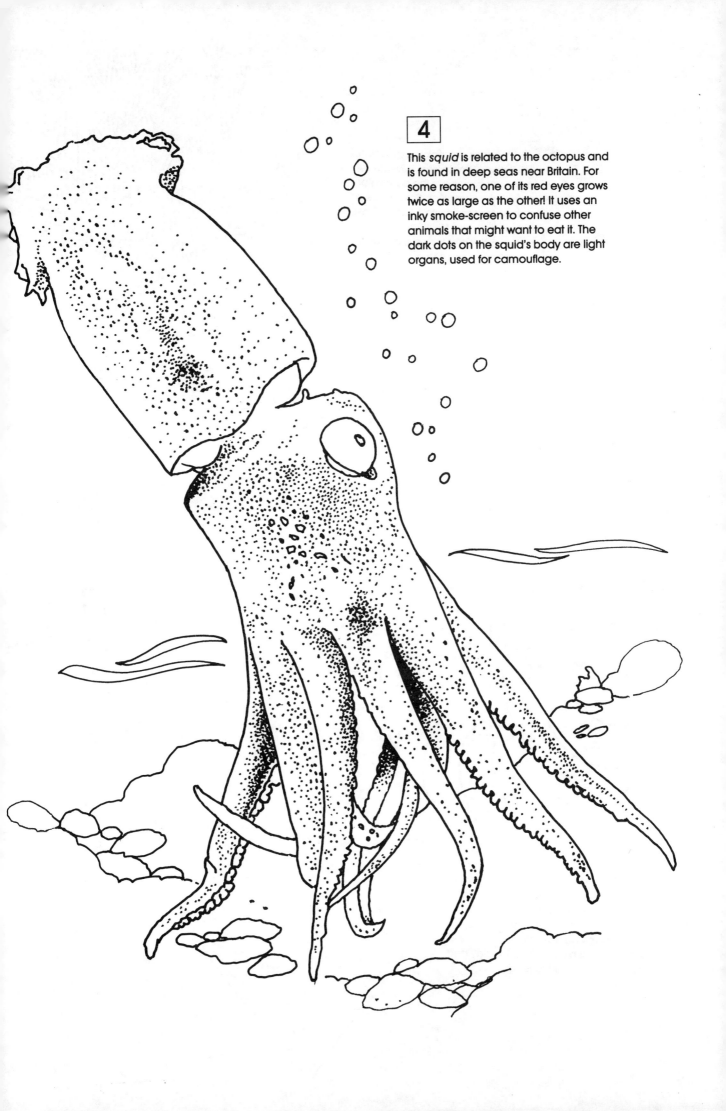

4

This *squid* is related to the octopus and is found in deep seas near Britain. For some reason, one of its red eyes grows twice as large as the other! It uses an inky smoke-screen to confuse other animals that might want to eat it. The dark dots on the squid's body are light organs, used for camouflage.

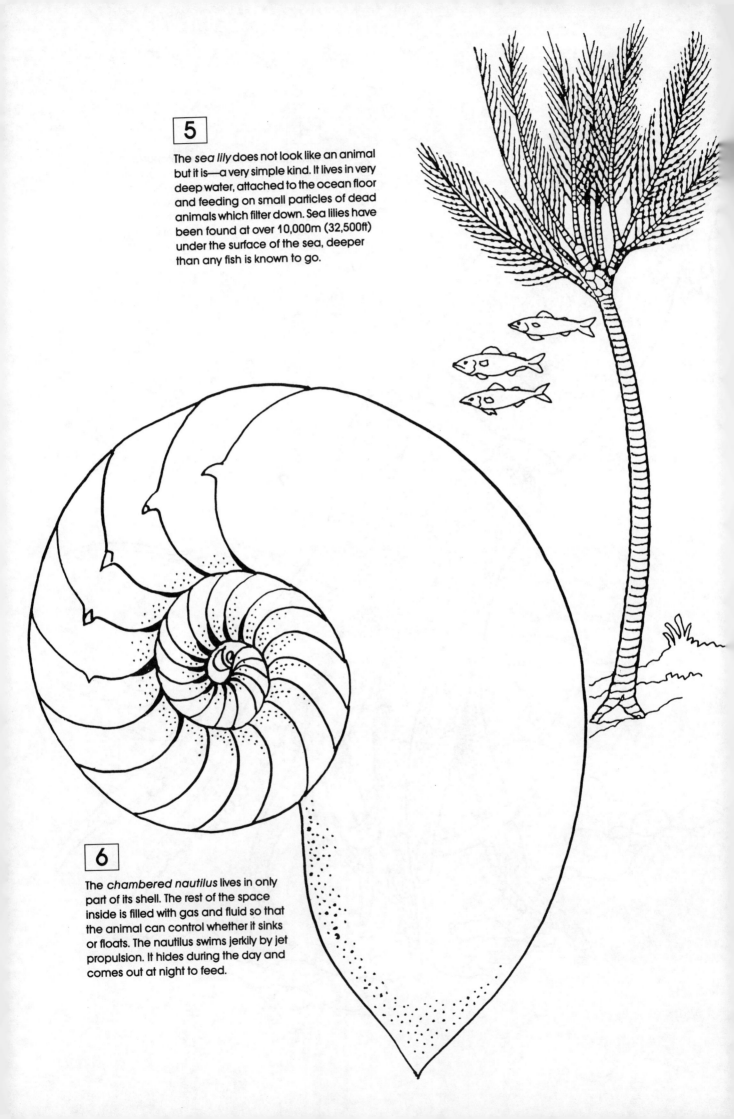

5

The *sea lily* does not look like an animal but it is—a very simple kind. It lives in very deep water, attached to the ocean floor and feeding on small particles of dead animals which filter down. Sea lilies have been found at over 10,000m (32,500ft) under the surface of the sea, deeper than any fish is known to go.

6

The *chambered nautilus* lives in only part of its shell. The rest of the space inside is filled with gas and fluid so that the animal can control whether it sinks or floats. The nautilus swims jerkily by jet propulsion. It hides during the day and comes out at night to feed.

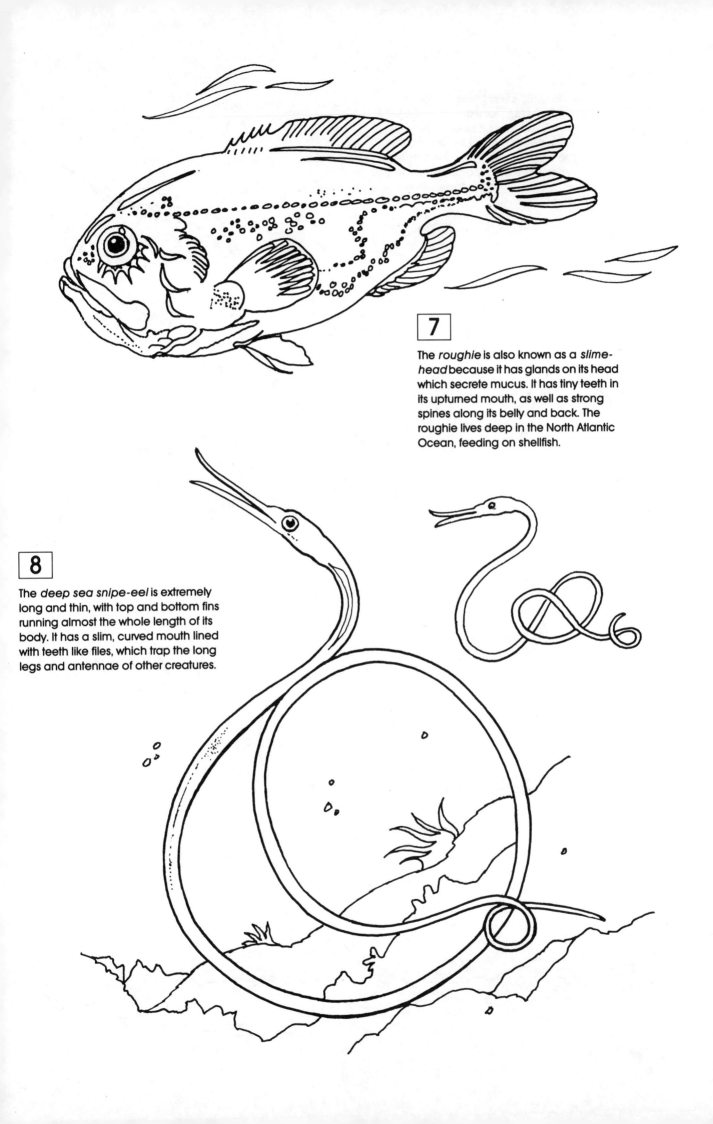

7

The *roughie* is also known as a *slime-head* because it has glands on its head which secrete mucus. It has tiny teeth in its upturned mouth, as well as strong spines along its belly and back. The roughie lives deep in the North Atlantic Ocean, feeding on shellfish.

8

The *deep sea snipe-eel* is extremely long and thin, with top and bottom fins running almost the whole length of its body. It has a slim, curved mouth lined with teeth like files, which trap the long legs and antennae of other creatures.

9

The *octopus* is very intelligent for an
invertebrate (animal with no backbone)
and we know that it can learn things. It
hides in crevices during the day, darting
out to catch its prey. When the octopus
is excited, its skin may grow darker and
even change its texture to match its
background.

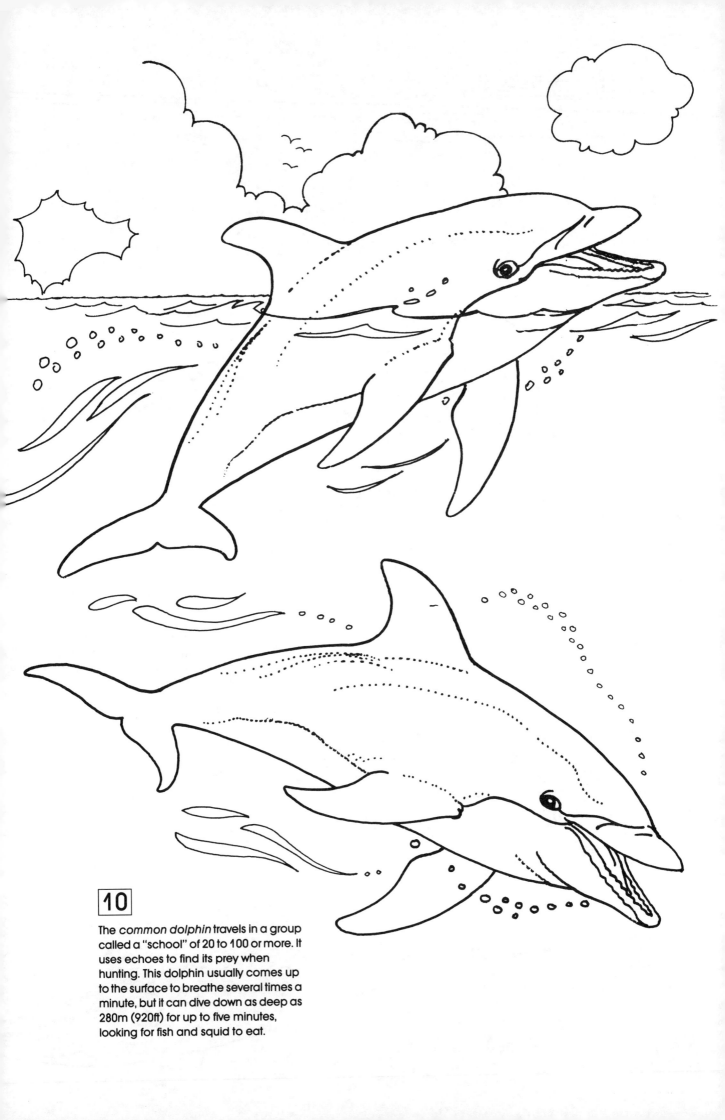

10

The *common dolphin* travels in a group called a "school" of 20 to 100 or more. It uses echoes to find its prey when hunting. This dolphin usually comes up to the surface to breathe several times a minute, but it can dive down as deep as 280m (920ft) for up to five minutes, looking for fish and squid to eat.

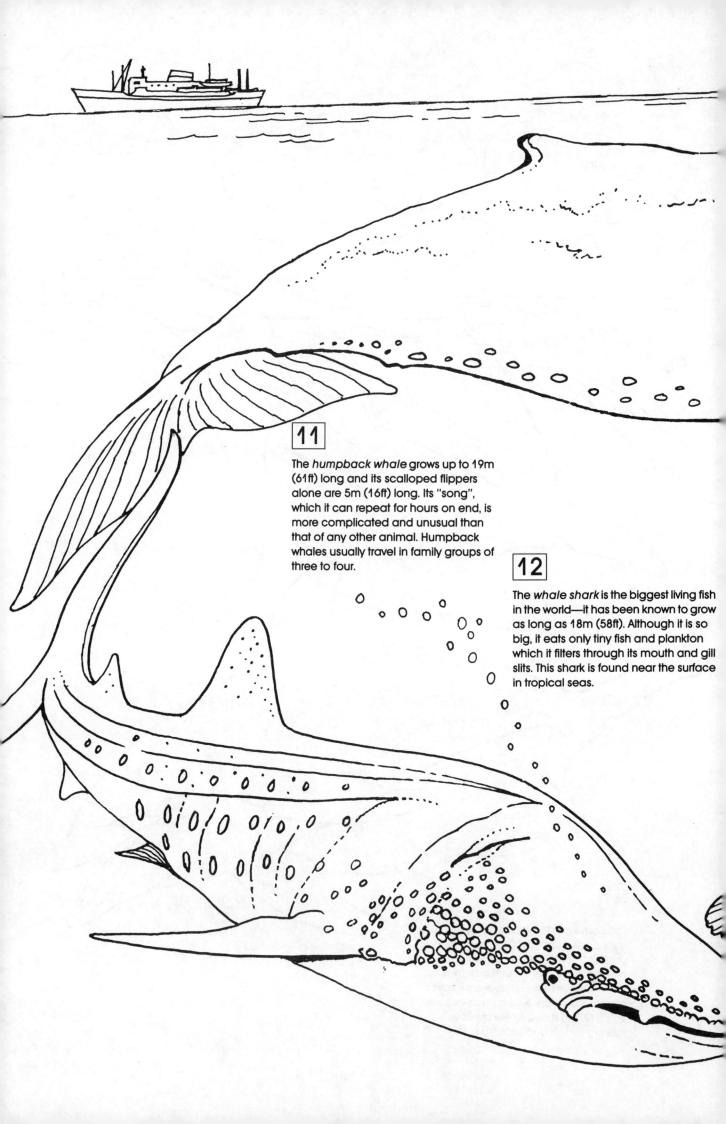

11

The *humpback whale* grows up to 19m (61ft) long and its scalloped flippers alone are 5m (16ft) long. Its "song", which it can repeat for hours on end, is more complicated and unusual than that of any other animal. Humpback whales usually travel in family groups of three to four.

12

The *whale shark* is the biggest living fish in the world—it has been known to grow as long as 18m (58ft). Although it is so big, it eats only tiny fish and plankton which it filters through its mouth and gill slits. This shark is found near the surface in tropical seas.

13

The heavy, slimy *coelacanth* is found around rocky slopes in the Indian ocean. It is thought to be the oldest kind of fish still living. It resembles many fossils and has helped scientists to learn more about extinct creatures. Some things about the coelacanth are still a puzzle.

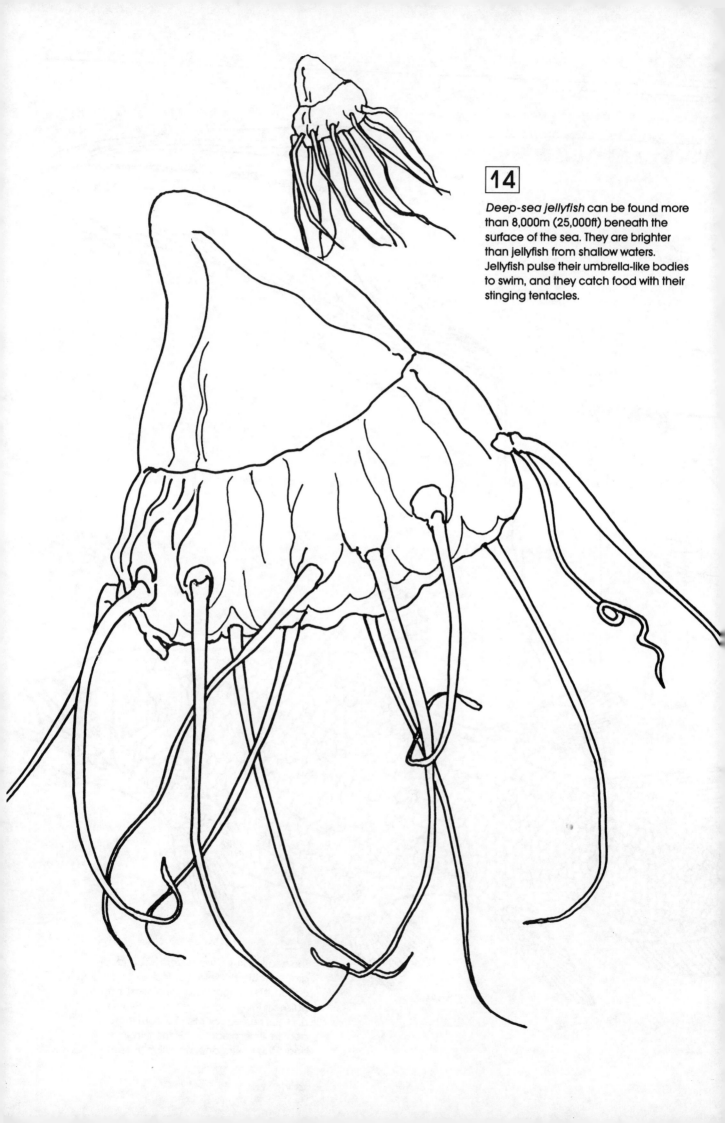

14

Deep-sea jellyfish can be found more than 8,000m (25,000ft) beneath the surface of the sea. They are brighter than jellyfish from shallow waters. Jellyfish pulse their umbrella-like bodies to swim, and they catch food with their stinging tentacles.

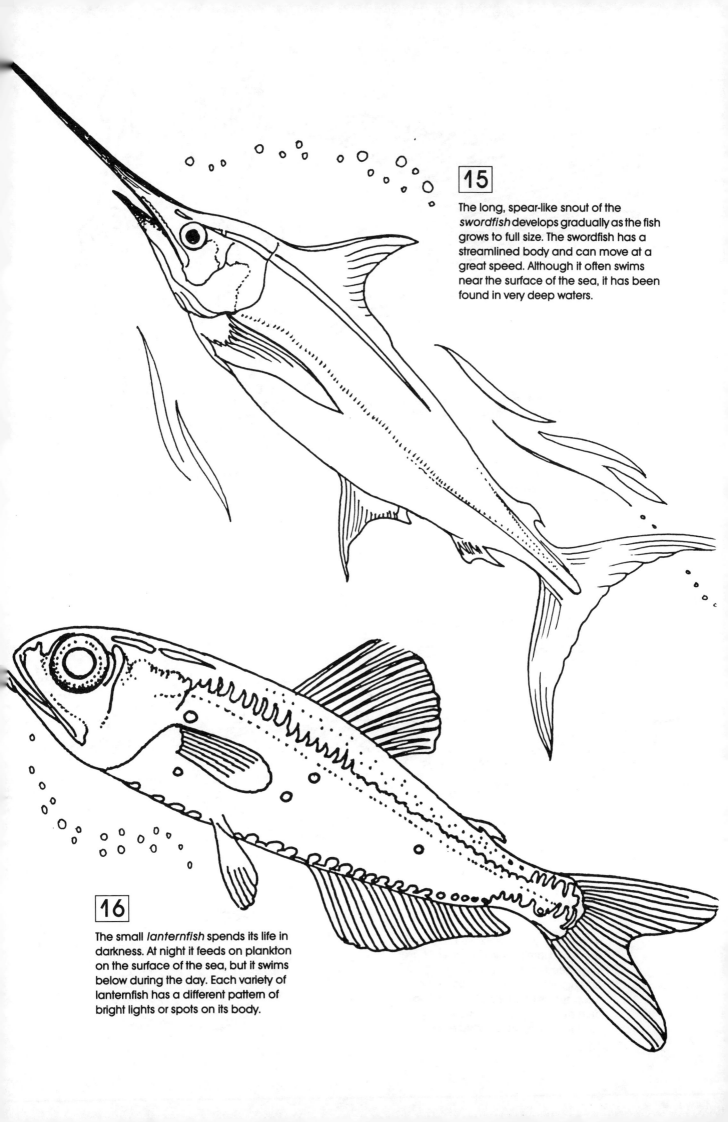

15

The long, spear-like snout of the *swordfish* develops gradually as the fish grows to full size. The swordfish has a streamlined body and can move at a great speed. Although it often swims near the surface of the sea, it has been found in very deep waters.

16

The small *lanternfish* spends its life in darkness. At night it feeds on plankton on the surface of the sea, but it swims below during the day. Each variety of lanternfish has a different pattern of bright lights or spots on its body.

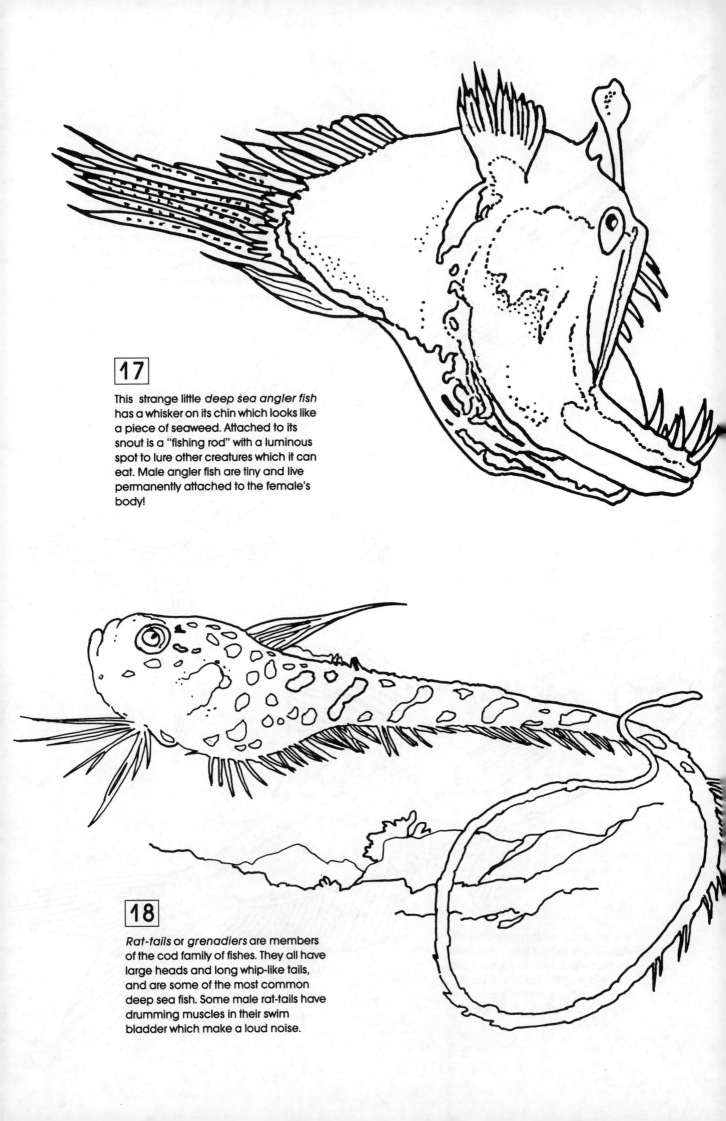

17

This strange little *deep sea angler fish* has a whisker on its chin which looks like a piece of seaweed. Attached to its snout is a "fishing rod" with a luminous spot to lure other creatures which it can eat. Male angler fish are tiny and live permanently attached to the female's body!

18

Rat-tails or *grenadiers* are members of the cod family of fishes. They all have large heads and long whip-like tails, and are some of the most common deep sea fish. Some male rat-tails have drumming muscles in their swim bladder which make a loud noise.

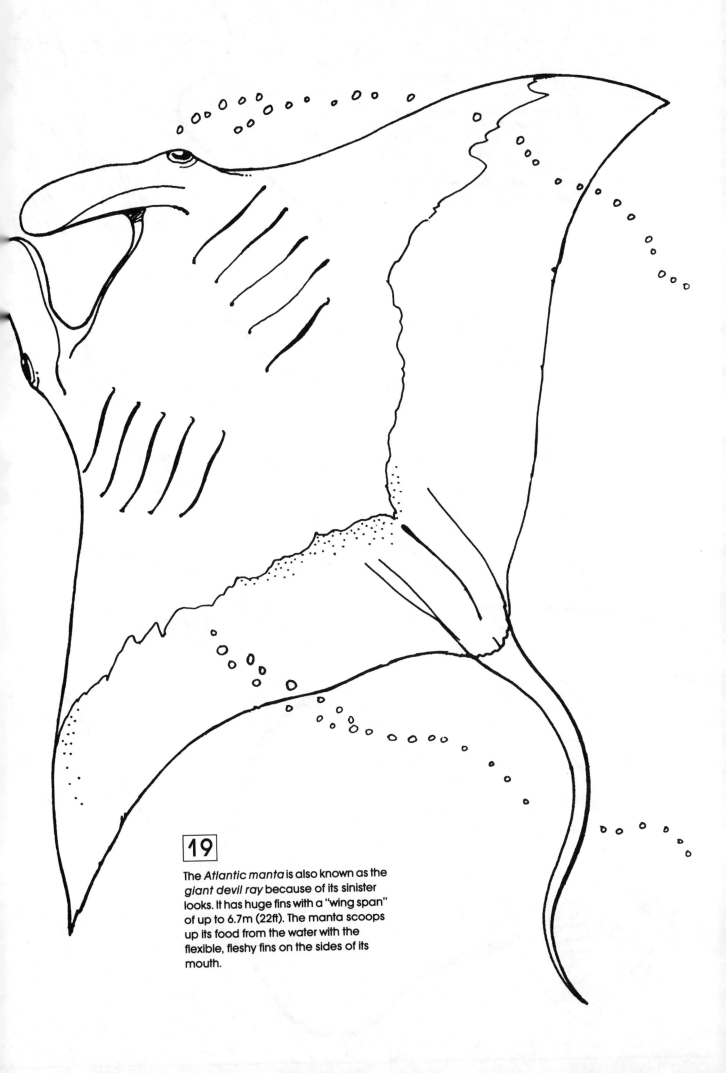

19

The *Atlantic manta* is also known as the
giant devil ray because of its sinister
looks. It has huge fins with a "wing span"
of up to 6.7m (22ft). The manta scoops
up its food from the water with the
flexible, fleshy fins on the sides of its
mouth.

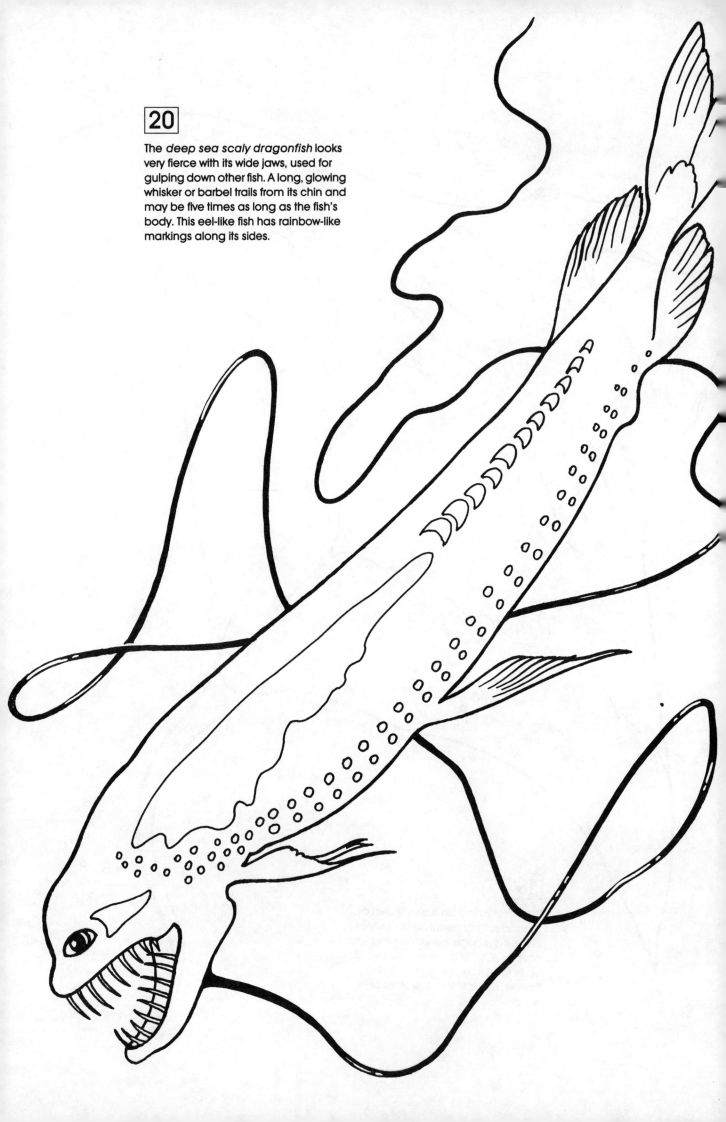

20

The *deep sea scaly dragonfish* looks
very fierce with its wide jaws, used for
gulping down other fish. A long, glowing
whisker or barbel trails from its chin and
may be five times as long as the fish's
body. This eel-like fish has rainbow-like
markings along its sides.

1

s *deep sea prawn* is found in the
oical Pacific. It lives on the remains of
ad creatures and grows to 35cm
in.). Only prawns living in the
rkness of the deep ocean are bright
d like this variety.

22

The thin arms of *brittle stars* may easily
break off, but they can grow new parts.
These animals move along the sea bed
by rowing with their arms, leaving trails
behind them in the sand. Deep sea
brittle stars catch tiny food particles on
their sticky tentacles.

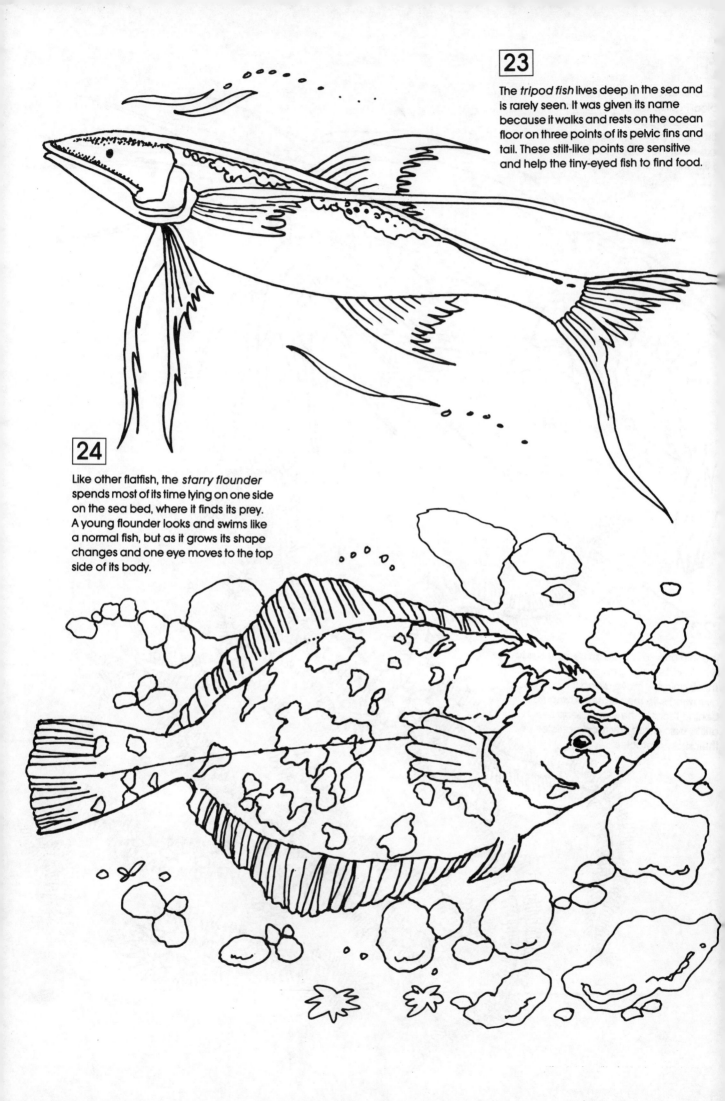

23

The *tripod fish* lives deep in the sea and is rarely seen. It was given its name because it walks and rests on the ocean floor on three points of its pelvic fins and tail. These stilt-like points are sensitive and help the tiny-eyed fish to find food.

24

Like other flatfish, the *starry flounder* spends most of its time lying on one side on the sea bed, where it finds its prey. A young flounder looks and swims like a normal fish, but as it grows its shape changes and one eye moves to the top side of its body.